DESMOND COLE
GHOST PATROL

THE HAUNTED HOUSE NEXT DOOR

by Andres Miedoso
illustrated by Victor Rivas

LITTLE SIMON

New York   London   Toronto   Sydney   New Delhi

LITTLE SIMON

An imprint of Simon & Schuster Children's Publishing Division
1230 Avenue of the Americas, New York, New York 10020
First Little Simon paperback edition December 2017
Copyright © 2017 by Simon & Schuster, Inc.
Also available in a Little Simon hardcover edition.
All rights reserved, including the right of reproduction in whole or in part in any form.
LITTLE SIMON is a registered trademark of Simon & Schuster, Inc.,
and associated colophon is a trademark of Simon & Schuster, Inc.
For information about special discounts for bulk purchases, please contact
Simon & Schuster Special Sales at 1-866-506-1949 or business@simonandschuster.com.
The Simon & Schuster Speakers Bureau can bring authors to your live event. For more information
or to book an event contact the Simon & Schuster Speakers Bureau at 1-866-248-3049 or
visit our website at www.simonspeakers.com.
Designed by Steve Scott
Manufactured in the United States of America 1119 MTN
6 8 10 9 7 5
Library of Congress Cataloging-in-Publication Data
Names: Miedoso, Andres, author. | Rivas, Victor, illustrator.
Title: The haunted house next door / by Andres Miedoso ; illustrated by Victor Rivas.
Description: First Little Simon paperback edition. | New York : Little Simon, 2017. |
Series: Desmond Cole Ghost Patrol ; 1 | Summary: When supernatural things start
happening in the house timid Andres and his parents just moved into,
next-door neighbor Desmond Cole, eight, comes to the rescue.
Identifiers: LCCN 2017016655 | ISBN 9781534410381 (paperback) |
ISBN 9781534410398 (hc) | ISBN 9781534410404 (eBook)
Subjects: | CYAC: Haunted houses—Fiction. | Friendship—Fiction. |
Moving, Household—Fiction. | BISAC: JUVENILE FICTION /
Action & Adventure / General. | JUVENILE FICTION / Imagination & Play. |
JUVENILE FICTION / Readers / Chapter Books.
Classification: LCC PZ7.1.M518 Hau 2017 | DDC [Fic]—dc23
LC record available at https://lccn.loc.gov/2017016655

CONTENTS

CHAPTER ONE

WELCOME TO KERSVILLE

When you move to a new town, grown-ups always give you a lot of advice. They say you should explore your new neighborhood right away. They say you should make new friends as soon as possible.

They never tell you what to do if your house is haunted.

Good thing I live next door to the coolest, bravest kid in the world. That's him, but he's busy right now. You would be too if a ghost was trying to slime you!

His name is Desmond Cole.

DESMOND COLE →

Me? I'm Andres Miedoso, and I'm definitely *not* the coolest and bravest kid in the world.

Do you see me?

ANDRES MIEDOSO

Look behind our brand-new sofa. That's my foot, and it's quivering with fear. Do you want to know why? Well, look up.

GHOST

Yep. That's a ghost. He's seconds away from sliming our brand-new sofa . . . and me!

But wait.

There's another thing grown-ups tell kids. They always say you have to start at the beginning.

It all began yesterday, when my parents and I moved to Kersville. We pulled in front of our new place, and the movers were already there with trucks blocking the driveway.

"Isn't it a beautiful house?" Mom asked, turning around in her seat.

"It's okay," I mumbled.

"I know you're nervous about moving, *mi hijo*," she said. "But there's nothing to worry about."

Mom and Dad got out of the car, and I followed behind them slowly.

That was when I heard something coming from next door. The garage door opened, and two boys came out. They shook hands, and one boy walked away.

"There's a boy your age right next door," Mom said. "See how lucky you are, Andres! Go and make friends."

Mom made everything sound so easy.

"Go on," Dad said. "Have some fun."

"All right," I mumbled.

That was when the boy next door waved to me. "Can you come over?" he asked.

I nodded and walked over. With his garage door open, I could see that it looked more like an office inside. There was an old desk, two chairs, and a bookcase full of thick books.

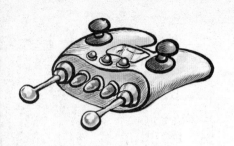

On the desk there was a flashlight, a video camera, walkie-talkies, and some weird gadgets with numbers on them. I started to get a little nervous.

"Hey," the boy said, smiling. "I'm Desmond Cole."

"Um, I'm Andres Miedoso."

"This is a great neighborhood," Desmond said. "Well, except for —"

"What is that?" I asked, spotting some odd-looking glasses hanging on the wall.

"Those are night-vision goggles," he replied.

"*Night-vision goggles?*" I asked, but Desmond interrupted me.

"Andres, I have to warn you."

Warn me? Now I was getting nervous.

"It's my mom," he said. "She's making a welcome lasagna for your family."

"That sounds nice," I said.

Desmond leaned in close to me.

"Don't eat it. Trust me. My mom is a pretty terrible cook." Then he laughed.

I tried to laugh too, but this kid and his strange garage-office were freaking me out. "Um, I'd better go now."

"Here," Desmond said, handing me a business card.

Desmond Cole

GHOST PATROL
No Ghost Too Tricky
Call 555-NO-GHOST

"Uh, um, thanks," I said, and slowly backed away. "S-see you around."

I ran home thinking about how much I never wanted to see him again. *Never.*

Of course, that was before I knew what it was like living in Kersville. Everybody needed a friend like Desmond Cole in this town.

CHAPTER TWO

NORMAL-BORING HAPPY

Mom and Dad were busy with the movers, so I decided to check out the new house. After meeting Desmond, I needed time to get my heartbeat back to its normal speed.

Even though there were boxes everywhere and the furniture wasn't

where it was supposed to be, the house was normal. Normal and boring.

A normal-boring front door and a normal-boring den.

A normal-boring kitchen and a normal-boring dining room.

There were four normal-boring bedrooms and two normal-boring bathrooms.

The front yard and the garage were . . . well, you get it.

The thing is, I like normal-boring. I understand normal-boring.

Maybe that's because I'm normal-boring too.

NORMAL-BORING HAIR

NORMAL-BORING MOUTH

NORMAL-BORING SHIRT

NORMAL-BORING JEANS

NORMAL-BORING SHOES

The only thing that wasn't normal-boring about this house was the basement. The stairs creaked as I walked down. It was almost completely dark except for a little light that came in from a small window. There were shadows everywhere.

There were also pipes that made clanging noises, and I jumped every single time they clanked.

I ran back
upstairs. Sure,
most basements
were creepy, but I
didn't want to take any
chances. I like the normal-
boring parts of the house,
thank you very much.

Mom was in the den. "Did you
get along with the boy next door?"

she asked me. "Wouldn't it be great
if you found a best friend on your
first day here?"

"Mom, nobody becomes best
friends in two minutes! That would
be a world record!"

"I just want you to be happy here
in Kersville," she said.

"I'm happy," I told her.
"And yeah, Desmond
is pretty cool."

She smiled.
"Good."

I didn't want Mom to worry about me, but the truth is, I wasn't sure Desmond Cole would make a good best friend. Something about him seemed . . . strange.

I went upstairs to my new room and started unpacking. I wanted my room to look the way it did in my last house and the house before that. Normal-boring.

Maybe Kersville would be as normal-boring as my room. But something told me I wouldn't be so lucky.

CHAPTER THREE

WHATEVS

DING-DONG! That evening, the doorbell rang. It was Desmond and his parents, and sure enough, his mom was carrying a casserole dish. I was super-hungry, but that was probably the lasagna Desmond told me about—no, *warned me about.*

Everyone introduced themselves and came inside. "I made this for you," Mrs. Cole said, handing Mom the dish. "Cooking is the last thing you need to think about when you move into a new house."

Mom thanked Mrs. Cole. Then she said, "Andres, why don't you show Desmond your new room?"

"Okay," I said. I knew she just wanted to talk to the grown-ups without us kids around. And that was fine with me.

On the way upstairs, Desmond stopped short. "What's wrong?" I asked, but he didn't say anything.

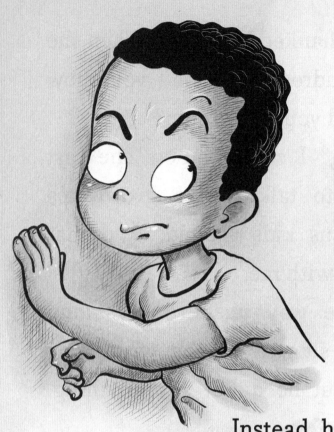

Instead, he tapped
the wall and put his ear to it.
My panicky feeling came back.
"Wh-what are y-you . . . ?"
"Shhh." He listened to the wall.

Then he blew out puffs of air all around. After that he licked his finger and held it up into the air. None of this made any sense to me.

"What are you doing?" I finally asked.

He shrugged. "Oh, sorry. That's just something I do."

"Okay," I said. "Whatevs."

We walked into my room. Covering one wall was a gigantic poster of the entire solar system. The poster was so huge it made my room feel like it was in outer space.

"Oh wow!" Desmond exclaimed. "That's the coolest thing I ever saw."

"Yeah, my dad got it for me," I told

Desmond. "It's the first thing I put on my wall whenever we move."

That poster made every place feel like home.

"You're a space fan, huh?" asked Desmond.

"What was your clue, Sherlock?" I asked, and we both laughed.

Desmond looked around the rest of my room. "So what brings you to Kersville?"

"My parents are scientists working on a top secret project for the government," I said. "Oops. I probably shouldn't have told you that."

"Wait, seriously?" Desmond asked.

I nodded, because really, it was true.

"Your secret's safe with me," he said. "It must be cool to have top secret parents."

"Yeah, but we have to move a lot," I said. "Normally, we don't even stay in the same town for a year."

"Kersville isn't normal," Desmond said. "When people move here, they stay."

"I hope so," I said.

That was when Mom called from downstairs. "Hey, Andres, Desmond's parents are leaving now."

Before we left the room, Desmond tapped walls and blew out his breath.

But this time,
he jumped back,
as if he saw
something.

"Huh?" was all he said. Then Desmond licked his finger and held it into the air again. "Uh, you still have my card I gave you, right?"

My heart beat hard. "Um, why?"

"Call me if you need me, okay?"

"N-need you?" I asked.

Desmond smiled. "Yeah, like if you want me to show you around. We have a new comic book store and

a bike park. With a bike like yours, I know you ride."

Back downstairs, Desmond left with his parents. But I couldn't stop thinking about those weird things he had done or what made him jump.

Most of all, I couldn't stop wondering why he thought I would need him.

CHAPTER FOUR

A HAND IN THE NIGHT

That night, we ordered pizza for dinner and had a picnic on the living-room floor. Most of our plates were still in boxes, and we were too tired to find them. "We'll save Mrs. Cole's lasagna for tomorrow," Mom said, and I secretly smiled.

After dinner, I went to bed earlier than usual. As I walked into my bedroom, I tapped the wall like Desmond had done. Nothing happened.

I laughed to myself. *What did I think was going to happen?*

Then I heard it.

TAP TAP TAP.

I covered my mouth with my hand and stood still, listening hard. I waited, as stiff as a statue, but the wall was quiet.

Finally, I let myself breathe again. *It's just my imagination,* I thought.

Not only that, I was dog tired. I climbed into bed and read a few pages of my favorite book, but even that  couldn't keep me awake. I fell fast asleep with the lights on.

I was freezing when I woke up. My eyes popped open, and I looked around the pitch-black room. I wasn't even sure where I was at first. Then I remembered: I was in my new room. *But why is it colder than outer space?* I thought. *And who turned off the lights?*

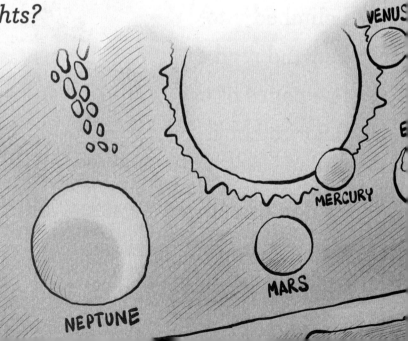

I blew out a huge breath of air, just like Desmond had done. In the darkness, my breath became a fuzzy white cloud that floated around my room. *That's not right.*

URANUS

TH

So I did Desmond's next trick. I put my finger in my mouth and then held it up. Bright blue sparks shot out from my finger, and shock waves ran through my body.

The lights started flashing *by themselves*, and when I saw my reflection in the mirror, I looked like a bolt of lightning had hit my head.

I sat there in bed, frozen with fear. That's when I heard a creaking sound coming from the walls. I dove under the covers—they were my only protection. Then something touched me. *It was a hand!*

"Andres?" Mom's voice was soft.

I peeked from under the blanket, and my heart skipped a beat. Mom was standing over my bed. She sat down.

"You were having a bad dream." She picked the book off my bed and put it on the night table. Then she leaned over and kissed me on the forehead. "Go back to sleep, and I'll turn off the light."

"Okay," I said. "Good night, Mom."

"Good night, *mi hijo*."

Sure, it's embarrassing that Mom had to tuck me in like a little kid. But after those crazy things happened, I did *not* mind at all.

CHAPTER FIVE

THE SILVERWARE MAN

The very next day was all about unpacking boxes.

And lifting heavy things.

And moving those heavy things to just the right spot.

While Mom unpacked clothes and books, Dad and I moved furniture.

Yeah, I was sweaty and tired, but I love putting things where they belong.

Dad and I saved the den for last. We had to lift giant chairs and a brand-new sofa, then set up the TV

and sound system. When everything was in place, we collapsed on the sofa, breathing hard.

Dad declared, "It's official. This house is our home. And to celebrate, we need my famous lemonade."

Dad thinks his lemonade is the greatest thing in the world. And actually, it is.

He went into the kitchen. As I followed him, there was a loud crash behind me. I spun around, thinking something fell over, but what I saw was . . .

How can I explain it?

In the two seconds my back was turned, the entire room had changed! All the furniture was rearranged, and the sofa was now floating, like, way up in the air.

"Dad! Dad!" I raced into the kitchen. "You have to see this!"

I grabbed him by the arm and pulled him into the den. But the furniture was back exactly the way Dad and I had arranged it. You never would have known anything had been out of place.

"What do I have to see?" Dad asked, sounding confused.

I just stood there with my mouth open. "Um, nothing," I mumbled. "I thought—forget it."

I couldn't tell Dad what had just happened. He would think I was losing my mind. Maybe I *was* losing my mind.

Dad shrugged. "Well, okay. Let's go get that lemonade. I'll bet you're thirsty!" He laughed and put his arm around me as we walked.

Mom had already unpacked the kitchen. It was normal-boring and spotless, just the way I like it. I tried to relax. "Everything is going to be okay," I told myself.

Dad was grabbing a pitcher from the cabinet when Mom called from upstairs. "Honey, can you give me a hand?"

"Okay," Dad said. "Lemonade when I get back, Andres. I promise."

I nodded and then closed my eyes. Maybe the den was just a weird daydream?

Then I opened my eyes and gasped. Every drawer and cabinet

in the kitchen was open. Cups and plates were piled on top of the table and counter, and our silverware was scattered on the floor.

I went to scream, but before the sound came out, the forks, knives,

and spoons all slowly moved around
in a circle. It looked like a tornado.
As they spun around, they started to
form into something that looked . . .
human. It was a . . .

...GIANT SILVERWARE MAN!

That was all I needed to see, so I took off and ran out the front door. I didn't even look where I was going. And as soon as I made it outside,

I slammed into something—no, *someone.*

I ran smack into Desmond Cole.

CHAPTER SIX

GRAPE SECRETS

"OOF!"

That was what Desmond said as I knocked the wind out of him. He sank into a heap on the ground.

"Sorry, sorry, sorry," I said, helping him back up. "I didn't mean— um, I didn't see you standing . . ."

"It's okay," Desmond said. "But seriously, dude, what's your rush?"

My mind was still racing from what I had just seen in the kitchen. No way was I going to tell Desmond what had just happened. No way was I going to tell *anyone*.

So I played it cool and searched for my calm voice. "I just, um, have to go to the store. You know, for my parents."

"Cool," Desmond said. "I'll walk you there."

"Okay."

On the way, I tried to hide how scared I was, but my legs were still a little wobbly. And my hands were still a little shaky.

I don't think Desmond noticed, though. He was too busy talking to people we passed on the street. It seemed like everybody in Kersville knew Desmond. One boy told him,

"Thanks for everything the other day."

"Glad I could help," Desmond said.

Then we passed a girl who said, "Hey, thanks, Desmond."

"Call if you need me again," he replied.

Finally, I had to ask, "What did you do for those kids?"

But Desmond changed the subject. "Did you eat my mom's lasagna yet?"

"Um, no, not yet," I told him. "We always have pizza the first night in a new home. It's a tradition with us."

When we reached the store, Desmond asked, "What did your parents want you to buy?"

I had no idea what to tell him. "I'm supposed to get, um, grapes."

The GREEN GROCERY

The GREEN GROCERY

The GREEN GROCE

Okay, I know that wasn't the best answer, but I could barely concentrate on what I was saying. My head was spinning with questions. *How did Desmond help all those kids? And*

why didn't he want to tell me? And what in the world was happening back at my not-so-normal, not-at-all-boring house?!

Then, almost like he was reading my mind, Desmond asked, "Have you discovered any secrets at the new house?"

Whoa, that was all I needed to hear. I was off running again, this time *away* from Desmond. Sure, I was making a complete fool out of myself, but I just wanted to leave him and his mind-reading questions behind.

I found the way back to my house, sprinted inside, and closed the door behind me.

That's when it hit me: I wasn't safe here, either.

CHAPTER SEVEN

THE FLYING TABLE

Inside the house, everything looked normal. The furniture was where it was supposed to be, and nothing appeared to be moving on its own.

Mom and Dad were hanging up pictures and asked for my help. They know I love hammering nails!

After the last picture was hung, Mom said it was time for lunch and asked me to set the table.

I walked to the kitchen as slowly as possible and peeked inside. Luckily, there weren't any scary silverware people.

As I put out plates, Dad poured his world-famous lemonade, and Mom heated up Mrs. Cole's lasagna.

Mom put the dish on the table, and that lasagna looked and smelled delicious. I wanted to dig right in, but I could hear Desmond in my head, warning me to stay away from it.

So I let Mom and Dad get some first, and I watched as they ate. They both took little bites at first, and then they started shoveling the food into their mouths, like it was the best thing they had ever eaten.

First I heard: "Ooh" and "Yum" and "Ahhh."

Then I heard: "Uh-oh" and "Oh no" and "Ugh."

That was when Mom and Dad sprang from the table. Their stomachs were making awful gurgling noises like tiny angry monsters. Then they ran out of the kitchen like two bolts of lightning and headed in opposite directions toward the two bathrooms.

Right away, both bathroom fans went on. But that didn't stop me from hearing way too many noises coming from inside.

"Ew, gross," I said to myself.

I pushed my plate away and got up from the table. On the counter, there was a bowl of—what else—grapes. I grabbed a handful and took a bite of one.

That was when I felt a cold gust of wind behind me. *What could it be now?*

I hoped it was just my mind playing tricks on me again. But it wasn't. What I saw was all too real.

The entire kitchen table—dish of
lasagna and all—was floating high
into the air.

I dropped my grapes on the floor
and screamed.

CHAPTER EIGHT

A Most Haunted Lasagna

As the table rose higher and higher, so did my scream.

I tried to move, but it took me a few long seconds to make my legs work.

Then, just like before, I ran from the room.

And, just like before, I opened the front door.

And, yes, just like before, Desmond Cole was standing there.

This time I didn't slam into him, which was a good thing because he was carrying some weird gadget. It made a whirring noise, and it had blinking lights.

I was shaking too much to talk, but Desmond had a huge smile on his face. "I knew it!" he exclaimed. "You brought a ghost with you, didn't you?"

He was so excited, he didn't even wait for me to invite him inside. He just pushed past me and ran into my house.

"What are you talking about?" I asked. "Me? Bring a ghost? *A ghost?*"

Desmond ran into the den and looked around. "Well, if you didn't bring it, then you're one lucky guy."

"Lucky?!" I said. Okay, this kid was bonkers.

"Yeah!" Desmond smiled as he waved his machine around. "Don't you get it? You are living in a haunted house!"

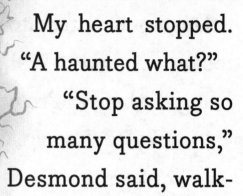

My heart stopped. "A haunted what?"

"Stop asking so many questions," Desmond said, walking through the den, pointing his gadget at the walls and the sofa and the TV. "Don't tell me you've never heard of a haunted house."

"I've *heard* of them," I said. "But I don't want to *live* in one. Can you do something about it?"

"Of course!" Desmond said.

"You moved to the haunted house next door to the right kid."

Desmond's gadget was making louder and louder beeps as he moved closer to the kitchen. I followed behind him. *Far* behind him.

"Whoa," he exclaimed, stepping into the room. "Does your table always fly like that?"

I shook my head. "Not usually."

"Good," Desmond said. "Because that would be really weird. But also kind of cool!" He didn't look scared at all. In fact, he looked like this was the most fun he'd ever had.

Desmond jumped up and grabbed one of the legs of the table and pulled it back down to the floor. We were face-to-face with the lasagna.

To be honest, it still looked really delicious.

"You didn't actually eat that, right?" Desmond asked.

"Not me." I motioned to the bathrooms. "My parents did and . . ."

Desmond shook his head and gagged a little. "Say no more."

Then without warning, the lasagna lifted out of the dish and floated above the table. I ducked behind Desmond and whimpered, "A haunted lasagna? Now I've seen everything!"

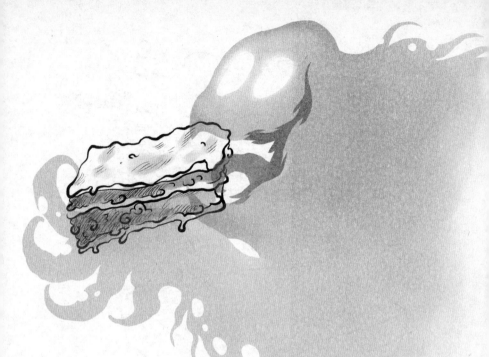

But I hadn't seen everything. Because when I looked again, the lasagna wasn't floating by itself. No. A ghost appeared out of thin air, and it was holding the lasagna in its ghostly hands. It sniffed the food with its ghostly nose and then gobbled the whole thing up with its ghostly mouth.

"This is not good," whispered Desmond. "This is not good at all."

Suddenly, the ghost turned green; puffed out its ghostly cheeks; and let out a loud, wet, disgusting burp.

It. Was. Gross.

If you've never smelled a ghost burp, consider yourself lucky!

"Ewww," I moaned.

The ghost puffed its ghostly cheeks again, but before it could burp again, Desmond yelled, "Run!"

And that was exactly what we did!

CHAPTER NINE

GHOST GUNK

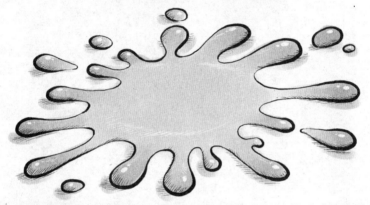

So here we are, where the story started. I wish I could say the ghost stayed in the kitchen. Or went back to wherever ghosts come from. But we weren't that lucky.

The ghost followed us into the den. And that's how I ended up here,

hiding behind the brand-new sofa.
Shivering and quivering.

Don't judge me,
though. You would be
hiding too if there was
a large gross burping ghost

floating over your head. The ghost
looked like it was going to be
really, really, really sick all
over the brand-new sofa.

And me.

Good thing Desmond was there. That kid wasn't scared at all. He looked up at the ghost and said, "Hello, I'm Desmond Cole, Ghost Patrol. You are in a home that is owned by this human, Andres Miedoso."

The ghost let out another burp, and this one stank even worse than the last. I covered my nose with my hand, but I could still smell it. That was when the ghost turned its head to look at me. I started to shiver and quiver at top speed.

"You own this house?" the ghost asked me in an eerie, raspy voice.

A ghost was talking to me.

"Um," I began. "My, uh, parents own the house."

"Are your parents human?" the ghost asked as it moved closer to me.

"Yes, I think so." I looked over to Desmond, who nodded and gave me a *duh* look, as if to say, *Of course your parents are human.*

Then the ghost turned back to Desmond. "What did I eat? It looked good, but it makes me feel so bad."

"I'm sorry about that," Desmond said. "My mom made it, but it wasn't for you."

"Is that what human food always tastes like?" the ghost asked, and it burped again.

"No," Desmond said. "Only when my mom makes it."

As the ghost
hovered above
us, I could hear
its stomach making the
same kind of monster noises
my parents' stomachs had made.

Desmond cleared his throat. "I know you are not feeling well," he told the ghost. "But I need you to leave this house. Do you have anywhere else to go?"

"No," said the ghost. It lowered its ghost eyes. "I move from one house to another all the time. I do not have a home."

Well, well, well, I couldn't believe it. I actually started to feel sorry for that ghost because I knew exactly how it felt to move all the time. Now the ghost didn't seem so scary. It just looked sad.

"Um, maybe you can stay here . . . in our basement?" I did not expect to hear those words come out of my mouth, but they did. "I mean, if you

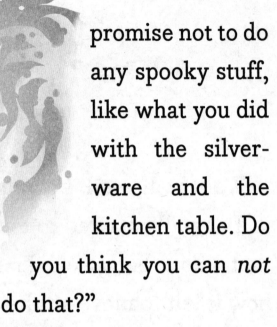

promise not to do any spooky stuff, like what you did with the silverware and the kitchen table. Do you think you can *not* do that?"

That was when the ghost smiled. "Yes! Yes! Thank you! Thank you!" It looked so happy. It raised its arms to give me hug and said, "I promise to always be on my best behav—"

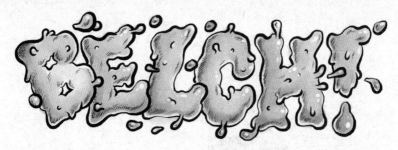

BELCH!

It was the loudest, ghostliest belch on the planet. It was followed by the ghastliest, grossliest gunk in the universe. And it landed all over our brand-new sofa.

And all over me.

CHAPTER TEN

MEET THE GHOST PATROL

Turns out, the ghost's name is Zax, and he's actually pretty cool . . . well, for a ghost. He tries to keep his promise and not scare me, and he never bothers my parents at all.

Actually, living with Zax is like having a little brother. He always floats through my walls uninvited, takes my stuff without asking, and reads my books before I'm finished with them. But I don't mind . . . most of the time.

Even if I did, I wouldn't say anything. Let me tell you, it's really hard to wash off ghost gunk. It's something I only want to do once!

As for Desmond, he's my best friend now. Even though he

couldn't stop me from being, um, slimed, he did solve my haunted house problem. Well, my house is still haunted, but now I know it's only because of Zax.

Life in Kersville is getting better and better. I have a ghost *and* a new best friend. Oh yeah, I have a new after-school job, too. I joined the Ghost Patrol. Desmond says it's easier with more than one person.

Right now, my biggest fear is that my parents will tell me it's time to move again. That would be the worst because I kind of really like it here.

Desmond gets calls all the time from kids who need his help—no, *our* help. That's what makes Kersville such an unusual place. You never know what's going to happen next.

And believe it or not, I like that.

Andres Miedoso
~~Desmond Cole~~
GHOST PATROL
No Ghost Too Tricky
Call 555-NO-GHOST